William W. Wheildon

History of Paul Revere's Signal Lanterns

April 18, 1775 - in the steeple of the North Church - with an account of the
tablet on Christ Church and the monuments at Highland Park and
Dorchester Heights

William W. Wheildon

History of Paul Revere's Signal Lanterns
April 18, 1775 - in the steeple of the North Church - with an account of the tablet on Christ Church and the monuments at Highland Park and Dorchester Heights

ISBN/EAN: 9783337391935

Printed in Europe, USA, Canada, Australia, Japan

Cover: Foto ©Andreas Hilbeck / pixelio.de

More available books at **www.hansebooks.com**

HISTORY

OF

Paul Revere's Signal Lanterns

APRIL 18, 1775,

IN THE

STEEPLE OF THE NORTH CHURCH:

WITH AN ACCOUNT OF

THE TABLET ON CHRIST CHURCH AND THE MONUMENTS AT

HIGHLAND PARK AND DORCHESTER HEIGHTS.

◄•◦•►

BY WILLIAM W. WHEILDON.

WITH HELIOTYPE OF CHRIST CHURCH.

CONCORD:
AUTHOR'S PRIVATE PRINTING OFFICE,
1878.

PRESS-WORK

BY RAND, AVERY AND CO.,
FRANKLIN STREET,
Boston.

TO THE MEMORY OF

JOSEPH WARREN,

WHO PROMPTED THE PATRIOTIC MOVEMENTS OF APRIL 18TH;

PAUL REVERE,

WHOSE FORESIGHT PROVIDED FOR THE SIGNAL LANTERNS;

ROBERT NEWMAN,

WHO DISPLAYED THE LANTERNS FROM THE CHURCH STEEPLE;

AND THEIR PATRIOTIC ASSOCIATES,

THIS VOLUME

IS RESPECTFULLY INSCRIBED,

BY THE AUTHOR.

INTRODUCTORY.

THE attention of the writer was called to the subject of Paul Revere's Signal Lanterns subsequently to the action of the City Council of 1876, in relation to a tablet and inscription to be placed on *Christ Church*, to indicate the place where they were shown. It was somewhat surprising that any doubt should be thrown upon the accepted history of that incident, either as to the place where the lanterns were displayed, the sole author and the purpose of them, or the party by whom they were shown. It is a satisfaction to know that that doubt has been dispelled, and it is now believed the true history must be considered as established.

In preparing the history of this interesting event, — preceding the expedition of Gen. Gage's troops to Concord, — the single question of the location of the signal lanterns, was by no means the only consideration. Statements and assertions, connected with this incident, or brought into the discussion, have been made, which, if any value is to be placed on the truthfulness of history and the honor of those who were engaged in making it, ought to be met and answered. Without particularizing any of these, some of which have been considered, the

sole aim has been to reach the truth, as clearly as possible, by
the light of the evidence now accessible.

At the second or third hearing given by the committee of the
City Council on the subject, in December, 1877, after a post-
ponement of the purpose for a year, the Rev. Dr. Burroughs,
Rector of Christ Church, offered for the consideration of
the committee some facts and opinions, included in the present
history, but necessarily in an incomplete form. Since that
time the history of the incident has been completed, and is now
presented for the consideration of the Council and the public,
and it is hoped that it will be found to confirm the action of the
City Council in placing the tablet upon *Christ Church* and
prove to be a correct and satisfactory account of the interesting
event which has been so suitably commemorated.

THE AUTHOR.

Concord, Mass., October 17, 1878.

ORDER OF NARRATION.

REVOLUTIONARY MEMORIALS.

On the 30th of March, Gage sent out several regiments under Earl Percy, to Jamaica Plain, across to Dorchester, and over the Neck into town again; and it was thought at the time they went out that they might be going to Concord, which it was supposed they soon would do.

1775. April 14. "If the enemy moves into the country, (which by all their manœuvres at present, there remains no dispute of,) the country are determined to oppose 'em; at least if they proceed in a hostile manner." [Andrews' letters, page 402.

"Dr. Warren, by a mere accident, had notice of it, [the movement of the troops towards the bottom of the common,] just in time to send messengers over the Neck and across the ferry to Lexington, before the orders for preventing every person's quitting the town were executed." [Gordon's History.

PAUL REVERE'S SIGNAL LANTERNS.

I. PRELIMINARY HISTORY.

It appears to have been the purpose of the late City Government to place a Memorial Tablet upon Christ Church, on Salem street, with the intention of indicating that as the building from which the signal lanterns of Paul Revere were shown, on the 18th of April, 1775; and this purpose seems to have been postponed by reason of some doubts thrown upon the subject by a recent communication addressed to the Mayor of the city.* The writer of this communication, for the information which he communicates and the conclusions which he reaches, relies upon "a memorandum, without date, in the hand writing of Richard Devens, made [as he supposes], not long after this period; in a letter written by Paul Revere, printed in 1789; and in various contemporary authorities," which are not mentioned. Of these papers, and the conclusions expressed, we propose to speak.

North End Mechanics.

It is well known that the abortive attempt of Colonel Leslie to seize the cannon at Salem, in the latter part of February, 1775, put the patriots of Boston on the watch for any new

---

* Letter to His Honor Samuel C. Cobb, Mayor, and Gentlemen of the City Council, by Richard Frothingham. Boston, December 28, 1876.

movement on the part of General Gage, and it was very early suspected that he had designs upon the cannon, stores and ammunition, at Concord, of which it was afterwards known, he was fully informed by the treachery of Dr. Church.

Paul Revere and about thirty other "North End Mechanics," in the Fall of 1774, formed themselves into a committee to watch the movements of the British soldiers, and held their meetings at the famous Green Dragon Tavern, until they suspected a traitor there. Towards Spring they took turns, two by two, to watch the soldiers by patrolling the streets during the nights. Revere says,

[April 15.] "The Saturday night previous to the 19th of April, about 12 o'clock at night, the boats belonging to the transports, were all launched and carried under the sterns of the men-of-war," and subsequently it was learned that "the grenadiers and light infantry were all taken off duty."

COMMITTEES OF SAFETY AND SUPPLIES.

On this day, at Concord, the Provincial Congress, which had been in session since the 22d of March, adjourned at the close of an afternoon session, which commenced at 3 o'clock. The Committee of Safety and Committee of Supplies, were also in session at Concord, and did not adjourn at the same time (Saturday) having important business before them. Mr. Devens was a member of Congress and of the Committee of Safety, and was present at Concord during the sessions of these bodies; but was not, at this time, Commissary.

FIRST MESSAGE TO HANCOCK AND ADAMS.

[Sunday, April 16.] On this day, in consequence of the discovery of the launching of the boats, (which had been laid up during the winter,) Dr. Warren desired Paul Revere to go to the residence of Rev. Jonas Clark, in Lexington, with a message to Messrs. Hancock and Adams, who passed their nights at Mr. Clark's house, while attending the sessions of Congress, at Concord, where, of course, accommodations must have been very limited for so large a body, as there were 216 members at Cambridge when the Congress adjourned to Concord. Revere, taking a horse from Charlestown, delivered his message as directed, and it is generally stated that Hancock immediately forwarded it to Concord; but this is probably a mistake.

First Idea of the Signals.

We come now to the origin of the signals : In the afternoon, Revere returned to Boston, making a stop at Charlestown, to leave his horse. It had occurred to him that if a movement of the troops should be made towards Concord, at night, it might be difficult for any one to cross the river from Boston to alarm the country, as the ferry boats were hauled alongside the man-of-war at 9 o'clock. In view of this, Revere says, "I agreed with a Colonel Conant and some other gentlemen, that if the British went out by water, we would show two lanterns in the North Church *Steeple*, and if by land, one, as a signal."

Mr. Devens, at this time was at Concord, and "in all human probability," never knew anything about this agreement with Colonel Conant ; and certainly never made any with Revere on his own account.

On Sunday night, after he got home, or Monday morning, Revere reported to Warren the performance of his commission, and made the necessary arrangements for the display of the promised signals, should they become necessary.

[Monday, April 17.] No further developments or movements, on the part of Gen. Gage, are reported, although the preparations must have been going forward unseen.

DOINGS OF THE COMMITTEES.

At Concord, however, the two committees of Safety and Supplies, most of whom had remained there over Sunday, (excepting Hancock, who went to Lexington, as usual,) were in session at Mr. Taylor's House. Messrs. Hancock, Devens, Heath, White, Palmer, Gardner, Watson, Orne and Pigeon, of the Committee of Safety, were present; and Messrs. Lee, Gill, Cheever, Gerry and Lincoln, of the Supplies Committee — fourteen in all, and those present proceeded to business before Hancock arrived. They " Voted that the two four-pounders now at Concord, be mounted, and that Colonel Barrett be desired to raise an Artillery company," &c. and also to " provide an instructor." It was then voted " that when these Committees adjourn, it be to Mr. Wetherby's, at the Black Horse, Menotomy, on Wednesday, 10 o'clock."

After these proceedings undoubtedly, Hancock arrived from Lexington, and he at once communicated the message which he had received from Dr. Warren — whereupon the meeting took very different action from that which they had already adopted. It was at once voted, " that the four six pounders be transported to Groton, and put under the care of Colonel Prescott."— [Col. James Prescott, who was a member of the Provincial Congress from Groton.]

" Voted, That two seven-inch Brass mortars be transported to Acton." And then it was " Voted, That the two committees adjourn to Wetherby's at 10 o'clock," notwithstanding the previous vote to adjourn over to Wednesday.

MEETING AT MENOTOMY.

"Menotomy, Tuesday, April 18th." The two committees met, and twelve of the fourteen members at Concord, were present : Hancock and Gill absent. At this meeting more than twenty votes were passed relating to the removal and disposition of cannon, ammunition, stores, &c. Part of the provisions were ordered to be removed from Concord and the vote directing powder to be sent from Leicester, to that town, to be made into cartridges, was reconsidered. Colonel Barrett was directed to bury the musket balls in some safe place, "and let the commissary [Pigeon] only be informed thereof."

As if having some idea of the events to follow, — soon after made probable, — the committees adjourned to meet on Wednesday at Woburn.

II. THE DEVENS MEMORANDUM.

Mr. Devens was present at Menotomy, and the "Memorandum" gives his account of his return to Charlestown, after a long absence, having but small knowledge of what was going on in Boston, and certainly none whatever concerning the signals which Revere had promised and provided for. The following is the memorandum in full :

"On the 18th of April, '75, Tuesday, the committee of safety. of which I was then a member, and the committee of supplies, sat at Newell's tavern, at Menotomy. A great number of British officers dined at Cambridge. After we had finished the business of the day, we adjourned to meet at Woburn, on the morrow, — left to lodge at Newell's, Gerry, Orne and Lee. Mr. Watson and myself came off in my chaise at sunset. On the road we met a great number of B. O. and their servants on horseback, who had dined that day at Cambridge. We rode some way after we met them, and then turned back and rode through them, went and informed our friends at Newell's. We stopped there till they came up and rode by. We then left our friends, and I came home, after leaving Mr. Watson at his house. I soon received intelligence from Boston, that the enemy were all in motion, and were certainly preparing to come out into the country. Soon afterward, the signal agreed upon was given : this was a lanthorn hung out in the upper window of the tower of the N. Ch. towards Charlestown. I then sent off an express to inform Messrs. Gerry, &c., and Messrs. Hancock and A., who I knew were at the Rev. Mr. ——, at Lexington, that the enemy were certainly coming out. I kept watch at the ferry to watch for the boats till about eleven o'clock, when Paul Revere came over and informed that the T. were actually in the boats. I then took a horse from Mr. Larkin's barn, and sent him ——. I procured a horse and sent off P. Revere to give the intelligence at Menotomy and Lexington. He was taken by the British officers before mentioned, before he got to Lexington, and detained till near day."

The reader will notice the loose and irreconcilable character of these statements ; the concluding mis-statement, and perceive that it is, what it purports to be, a mere memorandum of a most indefinite character. Referring to the time of the occurrences described, Mr. Devens says, "I was *then* a member of the committee of safety." As he was one of this committee until about July 19, the memorandum was not written within three months after the events at least. This makes the mistake con-

cerning the capture of Revere still more surprising, especially
as Mr. Devens was at Concord again, according to the date of
his letter calling congress together, on the 20th, and it would
seem, must have known what had occurred.

After he reached home Mr. Devens says, he " soon received
intelligence from Boston"; but as Revere brought over the news
to the party constantly on the watch for it, it is probable that
Mr. Devens's news came from them.   He also speaks of sending
an express to Menotomy, but did not furnish a horse, and probably refers to Revere, as none other has ever been heard of. —
He says, "I procured a horse and sent off P. Revere," but
Revere speaks of getting his horse before he met Mr. Devens,
and probably had the same horse he had used on Sunday. —
These, however, are not as remarkable as some other statements,
based on this memorandum, yet to be noticed.

MR. FROTHINGHAM'S STATEMENTS.

Mr. Frothingham says, " The setting of the lanterns was certainly an interesting incident of that evening ; but the facts
here stated [?] show that it was not the only warning of the
march of the British troops, nor was it the earliest warning."
No facts are stated, and none are known to us, to authorise this
last statement, so unjust towards that heroic and inde-
fatigable patriot, Paul Revere, to whom the whole honor of
the service, (save what Dawes might have done,) belongs.   Beyond all question "the setting of the lanterns" was the earliest
and "only warning of *the march of the British troops,*" and
as such, was carried all the way from Boston to Lexington. If
reference is intended to the express which Mr. Devens says he

sent to Menotomy, we think no express whatever started ahead of Revere, and if any started after him, which is not very likely, as we have said, was never again heard of.

The next statement is of the same character and no less untrue : " Then it was a private signal agreed upon between Paul Revere and Richard Devens." We have already annihilated this piece of fiction. Mr. Devens himself does not make or authorise any such statement. The agreement was solely with Colonel Conant and his friends, and Mr. Devens knew nothing whatever about it.

Mr. Frothingham makes another remarkable statement :— '' Meantime Devens at the ferry *saw the signals;*" but Mr. Devens himself is very careful not to say that he saw the signals, and it is very certain there is no other authority for the statement.

Mr. Frothingham makes some further statements, as follows : " I have no doubt that the lights of the lanterns   *   *   were seen by persons standing on the Charlestown side. The testimony to the fact is of a remarkable character. The earliest is that of Richard Devens. Paul Revere, in all human probability never heard of it." We think not.

These statements, like some others already quoted, are "of a remarkable character," to speak mildly of them. No doubt " the lights of the lanterns" were seen ; that is what they were put up for, and the remarkable character of the testimony is that no man tells us he saw them. The only direct evidence of the fact, earliest and latest, is found in the statement of Paul Revere, who says, when he '' met Colonel Conant and several others, *they said they had seen our signals.*" They told him they had seen the lights and he repeats the statement. This is all that has reached us. Revere does not say that he saw them, and Mr. Devens simply says, "the signal * * was given." If he had seen *it*, undoubtedly he would have said so.

We have thus seen where Mr. Devens was and how engaged until late in the evening of the 18th; who arranged for the signals, and why he proposed them; who saw and reported to him that they had seen them; what probable mistakes Mr. Devens made; what erroneous statements Mr. Frothingham makes, and have shown that the memorandum, as matter of history, is of small account. Mr. Devens wrote it a long time after the events mentioned, from what he heard and remembered,— not very carefully, we think,—and it is not to be regarded as of prior authority. The statements founded upon it, of which we have spoken, are not only wrong and unjust towards Paul Revere and Dr. Warren, but almost equally so to Mr. Devens, who was engaged on important public business at Concord and Menotomy, and did not know what was going forward in Boston, on the 18th, until he heard the news brought over by Paul Revere. But how such an indefinite paper, without either date or signature, can be exalted to the position so persistently claimed for it, — *and assertions made on its omissions,* — we are unable to see. The globose statement that Paul Revere never heard of this famous memorandum, is entirely gratuitous, and of no possible consequence to him or to the history of the event. The interesting question, as to the place where the lights were shown, is not in any degree affected by the memorandum or the statements purporting to be based upon it.

III.   PAUL REVERE'S NARRATIVE.

THIS important personal narration of the events preceding and relating to the march of the British troops to Concord, is held to be a *second* authority, subordinate to the memorandum which we have disposed of.   But in no sense is the memorandum of equal authority with the narrative of Paul Revere, which stands alone as the authentic history of the events of the period. Without this, and on the Devens memorandum only, Dr. Warren's presence would not appear ; the launching of boats and movement of troops not known; no message sent to Hancock and Adams on Sunday ; no signals proposed or agreed upon, and if seen, not understood ; no movement known until Revere arrived and " informed that the T. were actually in the boats," when Mr. Devens appears and adds the climax, " I procured a horse and sent off P. Revere to give intelligence at Menotomy and Lexington."* This would be the history as authorized by the memorandum, if that were ' prior authority ;' essentially incomplete and untruthful, with its real actors, — Warren, Revere, Dawes, Conant and others, — wholly ignored excepting Revere, who is made the messenger of the author of the memorandum. Warren, who had absented himself from Congress to watch the movements of Gen. Gage, and who prompted all that was done to warn and alarm the country in this crisis, and was killed before the memorandum was written, would not appear in the history at all.   The truth is Revere's narrative, instead of being

---

* " I told them what was acting, and went to get me a horse."   [Revere.

a second authority, is in fact, the only authority; furnishes the whole history, and is the means of securing to Warren the honor that belongs exclusively to him, and which his biographer has allowed another person partially to appropriate to himself. It may be true that Mr. Devens, who makes no allusion to Dr. Warren, in the matter, "knew what he was talking about" in his account of the British officers, seen on the road; but it is pretty clear, we think, that this compliment must be denied, when he speaks of sending Paul Revere to Menotomy and Lexington, as his messenger, and of his seizure.

SECOND MESSAGE TO LEXINGTON.

On Tuesday evening, 18th, (while Mr. Devens was riding from Menotomy to his home in Charlestown) at near 10 o'clock, Dr. Warren, having discovered the purpose of Gen. Gage, sent "in *great haste*," Revere says, "for me, and *begged* that I would immediately set off for Lexington." He went at once and directed the placing of the lanterns in the steeple; supplied himself with coat and boots; took his boat which he kept at the north end, and two men rowed him over to Charlestown. He then says —

"They landed me on the Charlestown side. When I got into town, I met Colonel Conant and several others; THEY SAID THEY HAD SEEN OUR SIGNALS. I told them what was acting, and *went to get me a horse. I got a horse of Deacon Larkin.*" While he "went to get a horse," the news reached Mr. Devens, who is now for the first time mentioned by Revere.

MEETING WITH MR. DEVENS.

"While the horse was preparing," says Revere, "Richard Devens, who was one of the Committee of Safety, *came to me and told me* that he came down the road from Lexington after sundown that evening ; that he met ten British officers all well mounted and armed, going up the road."

This appears to be all that Revere and Devens had to do with each other, somewhat differently related, and not only sets at naught the wholly unfounded assertion that the lanterns were "a private signal agreed upon between Paul Revere and Richard Devens," but corrects some other statements in the memorandum, and shows that the signal lanterns, in conception and arrangement, were exclusively the work of Paul Revere.

The points of Revere's narrative concerning the signals, are 1, his proposition and promise to Col. Conant to make them ; 2, the place where he would make them, and 3d, that they were seen by those for whose information they were intended : all these points rest exclusively, as we have seen, upon his testimony. There is no conflict of evidence in regard to them ; no question of their truthfulness; no other account of the events described, and that is undoubtedly the reason of his writing the narrative when he did, for the historical society. Revere was the only person, excepting those employed by him, who knew of his arrangements or could give any account of them. The narrative was printed in 1798, while he held the position of Grand Master of the Grand Lodge, which was held by Warren when Revere was his messenger.

Not a word, we think, is to be added to this history, and that which has been added to it is not true. We have evidence that the signals were made as promised, and were seen, and the purpose of them, if anything had happened to Revere, would have been accomplished through their instrumentality.

IV. THE NORTH CHURCHES.

THERE were during the period referred to in this history four churches, or meeting-houses, at the North End, which were respectively called, or spoken of and known, at some time, as the North Church, the new North Church, or the old North Church, namely :

1. The first of these in the order of time, was established in 1648, as the Second Church. This was on North Square ; was burnt in 1676 ; rebuilt in 1677, of wood, and was destroyed by the British soldiers, by order of General Howe, in 1775-6, and was not rebuilt.* This was known as the North Church in 1722 and 1732, and later than this, "the old North Church." After its destruction, the society in 1779, went to the New Brick, with their pastor, Dr. Lathrop, in Hanover street, (then Middle street), and the two formed one society. As Dr. Lathrop's was the senior society, or perhaps the largest society, they retained their designation as the Second Church and preserved the name of "the Old North Church," and thus absorbed the New Brick.

---

* December 11, 1775, General Howe ordered the troops to take down the old north meeting-house for the lumber [to build barracks], and a hundred old wooden dwelling-houses and other buildings for fuel."

1776, January 16. The Old North Meeting-house pulled down by order of General Howe, for fuel for refugees and tories.—[Newell's Journal.

In both these quotations it is called "the old north meeting-house," and we think was very seldom called simply "the north church."

2. The New North Church, 1714. This was on the corner of North and Clark streets, — a house of small dimensions, — Rev. John Webb, pastor; taken down in 1802, and rebuilt as now. Peter Thatcher was settled here as colleague with Mr. Webb, in 1720, and this produced a dissension which resulted in the building of the New Brick Church. Strictly speaking this was never called the North Church, but was known as the New North Church, and scarcely needs to be mentioned in this connection on account of its location.

3. The New Brick Church was finished for dedication, May, 1721. It was located on Middle street, and in 1779, four years after Revere's great exploit of April, 1775, was absorbed by "the Old North Church," taking its pastor, its rank and its name. [Paul Revere was a member of the New Brick Church in 1763, and of course of the Old North Church, by the union of 1779; but never was a member of the society in North Square.] In October, 1779, it was invited to the ordination of Rev. Mr. Eckley, as "*the north church*, under the pastoral care of Rev. Mr. Lathrop"; and at a later period, a sermon bears the imprint "By John Lathrop, D. D., pastor of *the Old North Church*." So the fact cannot be questioned that after the union in 1779, the New Brick church became the Old North church; but was never so called when Revere caused his lanterns to be shown in the *North Church Steeple.*

4. Christ Church, in Salem street, was formed in 1722. — This church was called "the North Church" very naturally by the denomination to which it belonged; and this title came to be recognized very generally by the public, a large part of the

people at this time, rigidly discriminating between a church and a meeting-house. It was spoken of as the "North or Christ church," in 1723. In 1768, Rev. John Graves, of Providence, wrote of it as "the North Church in Boston, where the late Dr. Cutler was their long and faithful pastor." Mr. Wm. H. Montague, still living in Boston, whose father was pastor of the church in 1792 and previously, says "I have always heard my father call the Episcopal Church in Salem street, the North Church." Mr. Abbott Lawrence, in a letter before us, dated August, 1846, expresses the "reverence he entertains for that good old structure 'the North Church,' as it was called when I was a boy." But there is no need of multiplying evidence on this point, which is not now disputed. It is beyond a doubt that at the time of the lanterns, Christ Church was generally spoken of and known as the North Church, but not as the old North Church, a phrase which belonged exclusively for many years to the old meeting-house in North Square, and afterwards to the New Brick church.

In the steeple of one of these churches, it is certain, the signal lanterns ordered by Revere, were shown; and it so happens that "the old North meeting-house," in which some persons believe the lanterns were displayed, was the only church of the four that was without a steeple, a fact which seems not heretofore to have been allowed its proper weight.

V. THE QUESTION CONSIDERED.

THE "Second, or Old North Church," meaning the old meeting-house, in North Square, not only never had a steeple, but from its location and want of height, was in no respect adapted for the purpose in view. The principal reason now, or ever offered, for supposing that the belfry of this meeting-house was used by Revere, is that it was known at the time as "the North Church;" generally, however, with the prefix *old*, as in the contemporary quotations and in Gen. Howe's orders "to take down the old north meeting-house." Excepting the force of this construction there is not a word that refers to this church, either contemporary or traditionary, and on this slender basis the claim in its behalf has been set up. Paul Revere does not say "the old North church," but the "*North Church Steeple*," and if anybody in America, at that time, knew what a "steeple" was, and would not confound it with "tower" or "belfry," that man was Paul Revere. — When he said "North Church *Steeple*," therefore, it is certain that he did not mean the "Old North meeting-house" belfry ; and this view would seem to be decisive of the question.

REVERE'S VIEW OF BOSTON.

Now it so happens that, in 1774, Paul Revere engraved for the Royal American Magazine, for January, "A View of the town of Boston, with several ships of war in the harbor," and in this engraving the belfry of the Old North meeting-house, the towering steeple of the North church, and the lesser steeples of the New North and the New Brick, are all shown : their location, relations to each other, and their adaptation in these respects to the purpose which Revere had to accomplish, will be readily seen and understood. No man knew better than Revere did the object in view, and to suppose that he would take a wholly inferior means — the least conspicuous of the four — when the best possible place for his purpose was open to him, is neither reasonable or probable, or consistent with the character of the man. We think it absolutely certain, therefore, that the belfry of the North Square meeting-house, was not the place used by Paul Revere for his signal lanterns, but the steeple of the Salem street church, which was by far the most eligible for his purpose, and remains so to this day.

BRITISH TROOPS IN NORTH SQUARE.

In addition to this it is very positively stated that the lanterns could not have been shown from the "old North meeting-house," for the reason that British troops were stationed in North Square at the time, and the act would have been seen at once and the party arrested. If this statement be correct, — and there might have been a small guard there as in other parts of the town, — the fact goes very strongly to confirm the conclusion already expressed.*

---

* We think there is no definitive mention of British troops in North square at the time referred to. According to Col. Wm. Heath there were in Boston, on the 20th of March, 1775, 2,850 troops, disposed as follows : on the Common, 1,700 ; at Castle William, 330 ; on Fort Hill, 400 ; at the Neck, 340 ; in King [State] street, 80. In June following there were over ten thousand troops in the town.

DISMISSAL OF REV. DR. BYLES.

It has been suggested that the Salem street church, being Episcopalian, was under English or tory influence, and could not be had for Revere's purpose. There is abundant evidence that this was not the case in addition to the fact of the dismissal of their high tory pastor, when, as he wrote to a friend afterwards, much " implacable temper was exhibited." He was dismissed on the very day on which the signals were displayed in the evening, and as only a few families continued in the town, the church was closed until after the evacuation. He says, in a letter dated October 7, 1775, " I still offered to officiate to them so long as I continued in Boston, but they treated my kind proposal with neglect. They chose rather to shut up the church, nor has it since been opened for a single Sunday. Indeed it is now scarce worth while to attempt it — most of them having left town — not more than six or seven families remaining." [The tory families remained in town, and finally went to Halifax.] Dr. Byles says, " Though shut out from my own church, I frequently assist at the other churches of the town, and there are several large hospitals of the sick and wounded, which I visit every week." These were British hospitals in Boston. A national patriotic prayer was adopted by the same parishoners when they returned to town and the church was again opened.

NEW BRICK CHURCH STEEPLE.

In looking upon the engraving of Paul Revere, it will be seen how little available for his purpose was the steeple of the New Brick church, which some persons believe was the steeple used by him, and which in 1789, was his church, and of which he was for years afterwards an active member : for wherever he was, he was active and prominent. This church, as we have seen, had become the Second church, and in virtue of this union, "the Old North church," and was so known when Revere's narrative was printed. It had a steeple which was superior for his purpose to the North Square belfry ; but at the time the lanterns were displayed, it had no claim whatever to the name of North church, while the Episcopal church, in Salem street, was always known by the Episcopalians as the North church, and among all the other denominations, this name was more or less common. It was the only available church with a steeple, that could have been in 1775, designated as the North church, and if Revere wrote correctly as to what he said to Col. Conant, the conclusion is inevitable that it was in the steeple of this church, and not in that of the New Brick, that the lanterns were displayed.

Again, if Paul Revere in writing his narrative, meant to designate the New Brick church, then the Old North church, as he very well knew, he would not have used the expression "north church steeple" at all, but would have said the "old north church," the "old north meeting house," or the old north belfry, the word steeple being entirely superfluous. The word "tower," used by Mr. Devens, and the word "belfry," by a modern writer, or the phrase "belfry-tower," used by the poet, can have no effect upon the accuracy of Revere's language, whether used as the equivalent of steeple or not.

In short, there is no reason to question the correctness of Paul Revere's narrative or the accuracy of his language ; and as we have shown, there is no other authority in the matter.

His statement we repeat as follows : " I agreed with a Colonel Conant and other gentlemen, that if the British went out by water we would show two lanterns *in the North Church steeple ;* and if by land, one, as a signal : for we were apprehensive it would be difficult to cross the Charles River or get over Boston Neck." He said "in the North church steeple," and the words cannot be made to mean a meeting-house without a steeple, or a steeple on some other church not suitable for his purpose. He states that Warren, when he sent for him, knowing of the movement of Gen. Gage, had already sent a messenger to Lexington, over the neck   He then relates how he got across the river, and was told that his lanterns had been seen ; how he procured a horse, as he had done on Sunday, and proceeded on his "Midnight Ride,"* so that his arrangement with Col. Conant, was completely carried out ; and, as we have said, the object of the signal lanterns would have been accom-

---

* We have not deemed it necessary to refer specially to the historical inaccuracies of the poet in describing Paul Revere's Midnight Ride. It is apparent, from what has been said, that the signal lights were not made for Paul Revere's information, but for Col. Conant and other gentlemen, (Mr. Devens included,) in case he should not be able to get across the river and spread the alarm himself : of course, then, the description of his standing on the opposite shore, "impatient to mount and ride," watching

—————— " with eager search
"The belfry-tower of the old North church,"

is simply poetry and not history. It is generally known, also, that Revere, after leaving Lexington, was seized and brought back without reaching Concord, and of course the lines —

" It was two by the village clock
" When he came to the bridge in Concord town,"

are the coinage of the poet. The alarm was given in Concord by Dr. Prescott, who had rather overstaid the evening with his lady-love, at Lexington ; and this might have furnished an apt episode for the poet.

plished had he been arrested or otherwise prevented from crossing the river that night.

The phrase "hung out," is used in speaking of Revere's signal lanterns as a common form of expression, but in this case
without authority.   They were undoubtedly "shown," as Revere agreed, and not hung at all.   Mr. Newman had no means
of hanging them, and no doubt held them in his hands with
out-stretched arms, for a few minutes only, scarcely, if at all,
outside the wall of the steeple — so that it is certain Col.
Conant and his friends must have been looking for them, and
knowing the location of the North church, knew precisely where
to look.   They were probably shown while Revere was crossing
the river below the ferry, which would bring the top of Snow
Hill between him and the steeple; or they may have been displayed while he was getting his boots and finding his men.   The
fact that they were so promptly shown proves that they had been
previously provided for and access to the church secured without seeking the sexton at that time of night for the keys.   We
very much doubt also if anybody else, other than those on the
watch at Charlestown, saw the lanterns at all, and it remains to
be discovered how Gen. Gage, or the British authorities, knew
of them, if, in fact, they did know of them when they were
shown.   Stedman, the English historian, makes no allusion to
them ; Gordon does not mention them, but says, "When the
corps was nearly ready to proceed on the expedition, Dr. Warren, by a mere accident, had notice of it just in time to send
messengers over the neck and across the ferry to Lexington, before the orders for preventing every person's quitting the town
were executed."   Neither of these authors mentions any pro-

ceedings in consequence of the display of the lanterns, as both
would have done had any taken place in the town.   Newell, in
his Diary, does not mention anything about the lanterns or signal of any kind; and Andrews, in his letters, simply says, the
" men appointed to alarm the country upon such occasions got
over by stealth as early as they could and took different routes."
Each of these writers gives the particulars of whatever occurred
in the town, and the slightest occurrences did not escape their
notice.   It seems almost impossible that the British could have
taken any notice of the affair without the knowledge of these
writers, or without mention of it by Gen. Gage himself in some
of his letters.

In Conclusion.

Whoever inclines to take the trouble to repeat Col. Conant's
observation from the end of the present old bridge, near where
the ferry was, on the Charlestown shore of the river, will not
be likely to doubt for a moment, that the lanterns were shown
from the *North* [Christ] *Church steeple.* Or let any person look from almost any elevated position in Boston, sufficient-
ly commanding for the purpose, as from the State House, City
Hall, or the Life Insurance Company's building, in Liberty
Square, or better still, from the North Church steeple, and he
will be satisfied of the same thing.   There was not then any
other place from which they could have been effectively shown,
nor is there so secure and eligible a place for the same purpose
within the limits of the city today.

VI. TRADITIONARY HISTORY.

Mr. Frothingham has no doubt that the "lights of the lanterns * * were seen by persons standing on the Charlestown side of the ferry"; "the testimony to the fact is of a remarkable character;" "the earliest is that of Richard Devens;" Paul Revere, "in his letter printed in 1798, mentioned the same fact; both agree substantially;" and the writer adds to these curious assertions this remark: "This constitutes historical evidence of a very high character. Tradition cannot stand against it."

There is nothing in these statements for tradition to stand against; to prove or disprove. They indicate that the lanterns were shown and were seen, and beyond this they are of no particular account. Revere said he would show, in one event, "two lanterns in the *North Church steeple*," and did so. Mr. Devens says the signal was given, "a lanthorn hung out in the upper window of the tower of the N. Ch. towards Charlestown." Here we have a difference of statement: "Two lanterns" *vs.* "a lanthorn," "steeple" *vs.* "tower." One of them knew what he was saying; the other repeated what he had heard. Revere does not say he saw *them* ; Devens does not say he saw *it.*— Revere's statement that when he "met Col. Conant and several others, they said they had seen our signal," is prior and positive evidence, as absolute as if Col. Conant had personally testified to the same fact. All other particulars depend upon tradition and inference.

What, then, is the tradition, or what is there for tradition to stand against ? The tradition is that when Revere left Dr.

Warren, he at once called upon his friend, Robert Newman, sexton of the North church, and " desired him to make the signals," as had been previously arranged, from the steeple. This statement, as far as the "steeple" and the "friend" of Revere are concerned, includes all there is of tradition, touching the showing of the signal lanterns; and this tradition, supported by and confirming the narrative of Paul Revere, after having been received, accepted and talked about, as veritable history, for a hundred years, has recently for the first time, we believe, been called in question and disputed in its most essential particulars. One of these, the question as to the church from the steeple of which the lanterns were shown, we presume, may be considered as determined, not merely by the action of the city government in the premises, but by a fair and reasonable interpretation of the language used by Paul Revere, and for other reasons which have been stated — all of which will be still further verified by the traditionary testimony which we propose to present. Possibly it may be found that the traditionary testimony is the strongest in the case, and is pretty much all one way, and that there is nothing for it to stand against.

Tradition, reasonably related, concerning events in times of secrecy and peril, is not to be slightly disregarded ; much of history may depend upon it or be confirmed and supported by it. The period of which we are speaking is not so very remote, and tradition comes down to us through a single generation ; men of most respectable character are living today who knew Paul Revere and Robert Newman, and have willingly testified of their information on this subject. These men, when boys, used to play together in Robert Newman's yard, on the corner of Sheafe and Salem streets ; and their uniform testimony is, that they lived at the North End, seventy or eighty years ago, and that they always heard and understood that the signal lanterns of Paul Revere were shown in the steeple of Christ Church, by Robert Newman, the sexton. This story was common with them and they never heard it contradicted. They never heard the names of any other persons, or any other church, mentioned in connection with the transaction, while the subject must have been a matter of frequent conversation in their presence and among themselves, during many years. We prefer, however, to state this matter more particularly in the language of the gentlemen referred to.

The Newman Family.

Robert Newman, the sexton, was the youngest son of Thomas Newman, a merchant and importer of Boston, who, becoming unfortunate in business, apprenticed his two younger sons, John and Robert, to trades, and when older they both became enrolled in the band of North End mechanics. John, who had a great love for music, became organist of Christ Church, and Robert, when the times became hard, took the position of sexton, which he retained during his life time. His youngest son being named after the Rector, Rev. Samuel Haskell, he desired to adopt the child when the father died. They were both freemasons, and after the war, Robert was an officer in Saint John's Lodge, and stood well with the prominent members of the fraternity, one of whom, Henry Fowle, became the guardian of his children. Revere and the Newmans were pupils in Master Tileston's school : playmates when boys, mechanics and patriots when men. Another brother, Thomas, was a manufacturer in England, and missed a fortune from his relative, Sir

Thomas Churchman, for whom he was named, on account of his
adherence to the cause of his native land. Some of his letters
exhibit very forcibly the strength of his convictions. In January, 1784, he wrote to his two brothers as follows, " After a
silence of many years, (occasioned by the rash, violent and
inhuman measures of a late execrable administration,) I take
the earliest opportunity to congratulate you on the return of
peace, and above all, the freedom and independence of my native
and injured country. A nobler cause than that which has
drawn the sword and fired the indignation of every worthy son
of America, is not to be found in the annals of the world ; a
cause that has been supported with a degree of firmness, valor,
judgment, spirit and perseverance almost without example ; a
cause involving the common rights of mankind, and the success
of which has occasioned inexpressible pleasure and heartfelt joy
in every free state upon earth." In another letter he says,
" your sentiments and mine respecting the American war are
exactly the same ; it was an infamous measure and has liber-
ated the country it was intended to enslave." In a previous
letter he speaks of the execrable war, and says Hancock and
Adams will be remembered after the British administration is
forgotten. There was no toryism in the family.

TRADITIONARY TESTIMONY.

Mr. Joshua B. Fowle, of Lexington, under date of July 28,
1875, writes to Mr. Samuel H. Newman, son of the sexton,
and says, " I have examined my memory and old records. There
is no dispute, or ought not to be, in regard to the display of
the lights at the North church by your father. The Seven
Bells church was always called by that name ; the others were

always called meeting-houses, old Puritanic names, and by no
other.   I knew in my young days many of the prominent men
who took an active part in the doings of those days.   Paul Revere lived near me.   I have heard it told over many times and
never doubted.   Any man is beside himself to entertain a
doubt.   I knew Henry Purkett, Major Melville, and others of
the Tea party, besides Revere.   It was common talk at my
father's, where they often met, although I can call to mind they
were careful of calling names, having some fear of liability,
which I a boy thought was impressed on them by the scenes
they had passed through."

In August, 1876, the same gentleman addressed a second
letter to Mr. Newman, and says, " It has always been known
to North End boys that Robert Newman was the man.   *   *
I knew Col. May, Capt. Green, Major Melville, Capt. Purkett,
and first on the list Paul Revere — a near neighbor to me — as
likewise Robert Newman.   *   *   Mr. Newman, as well as
Paul Revere, was educated at Mr. Tileston's school, and like
Revere, was a mechanic.   *   *   Mr. Newman was a man of
few words, but prompt and active, capable of doing whatever
Paul Revere wished to have done, and all these gentlemen mentioned knew of the act of Mr. Newman's displaying the lanterns, and if it were not so, they were the men to say so."

A letter from Jeremiah Loring, ninety-one years of age,
dated Chelsea. October, 1876, says he was born in Hull, and
resided in Boston 85 years, " heard in his youth the story of the
signal lanterns hung in the tower of Christ Church, by Robert
Newman, on the night of April 18th, 1775, from people who
were living at the time of the occurrence, and among whom I

never knew the truthfulness of the statement to be questioned. Robert Newman was personally known to me."

Messrs. Isaac H. Carey, Wm. L. Learned, Thomas Mair, Noah Lincoln, and William Parkman, all old residents of Boston, testify to the same general statement regarding the place and the person. Mr. Parkman says, he " often heard the story in his boyhood, and never heard the truthfulness of the statement questioned until within a week or two past."

Mr. John N. Barbour, of Boston, writes as follows : " In my early days I was deeply interested in the history of Christ Church. My grand parents occupied the house in Prince street, in which my father and myself were born and lived very many years. *   *   We boys always understood, in fact never heard to the contrary, that your father, Robert Newman, who lived at the corner of Sheafe and Salem streets, and in whose yard we so often enjoyed our youthful sports, hung up the signal lanterns giving information of the movements of our British enemies."

Mrs. Mary B. Swift, a resident when young at the north end of Boston, and now dwelling in Bowdoin Square, at the age of 84, a grand-daughter of Col. Conant, testifies that " when she was a young lady it was a frequent remark that the signal lanterns were hung immediately before the march to Lexington, by Mr. Newman, then sexton of Christ church, in its steeple, and that she never throughout her life, has heard it questioned until about a year since."

Mr. Mathew Binney, under date of Sept. 26, 1876, says, " I have always claimed to be a North End boy, born October 8, 1803 My home for the first twenty years of my life was the

estate owned by my father on the north side of what was then
Nos. 5 and 7, Salem Place, since widened and called Cooper
street. I have often heard in my younger days of the signal
lanterns having been hung in the steeple of the Old North
church, in Salem street, (or otherwise called Christ Church,)
giving information of the British movement in 1775. I have
always heard that they were hung by one Robert Newman."

The Hon Francis Brinley, formerly of Boston, in a letter
dated Newport, Nov. 22, 1877, addressed to Mr. Geo. Mount-
fort, says, " My grandfather attended Christ Church, *   *
and I lived as you know, within sound of the chime of bells.
I frequently heard the history of the church spoken of by the
senior members of the family, and have always believed that
the signals were hung on the spire of the church, as the most
conspicuous locality. I mean, of course, Christ church, in
Salem street."

In a second letter on this subject, Dec. 21st, Mr. Brinley
says — " My earliest recollections are of my childhood in
my father's house on the northerly corner of Prince street, op-
ening into Hanover street. The house was attractive especially
as to the somewhat ornate carving and arrangements of the
interior. There was a small garden in front on Prince street :
it has disappeared, and the house is almost obliterated. I
speak of the premises as I last saw them, several years ago."
" My grandfather, Edward Brinley, and grandmother, were
part of our family. He was educated an Episcopalian, and
worshipped at Christ Church, when the Rev. Mr. Walter was
Rector, who was succeeded by the Rev. Dr. Eaton, the projector
of the ' Salem Street Academy,' of which he was principal, and

the late Judge Willard Phillips his assistant. Of this school I was a pupil.

"Now, I recall three matters which were often spoken of in the family, connected with the church, which kindled my youthful imagination : one, the delicious Chime of Bells; another was the mad project of some *aspiring* man who proposed to fasten one end of a rope to the spire of the church and the other at a corner of Prince and *Back* streets, down which rope he was to slide upon a board; the third was the signal lights which were hung on the church just before the hostile meetings at Lexington and Concord.

"As my grandfather was a *Tory*, he naturally adverted to this subject. '*Christ church*' was sometimes called '*North church*,' even in those days. The other places of worship were called 'meeting-houses.' I have from boyhood believed these lanterns were suspended from *Christ church :* it was the nearest lofty edifice to Charlestown, and therefore most likely to be selected ; it was also the most northerly, and therefore was occasionally spoken of as the *North church*."

Miss Maria Green, living in Weston, born in 1793, is a daughter of William Green, who lived in Boston, near the *North Church,* where also her grand parents resided. She heard many times from her mother the story of the lanterns, and says, "I distinctly remember that she said her father, Capt. Thomas Barnard, was engaged on that night in watching the movements of the troops in order to obtain for Robert Newman the necessary information concerning their departure. Our family were familiar with the story of hanging out the lanterns owing to the connection of Capt. Barnard with it, and we never

heard the act ascribed to any other person than Robert Newman, or to any other place than *Christ Church.*" Mr. Green,
a brother of the lady above mentioned, who died recently in
Boston, is known to have made a similar statement.

Mr. Montague, son of the Rector of that name, (who is now
living in the Home for Aged Men, in Boston,) has heard his
father say that the lanterns which gave warning on the 18th of
April, 1775, were hung in Christ Church.

Thus we have given, as briefly as possible, the traditionary
testimony concerning Paul Revere's signal lanterns, the place
where they were shown and by whom displayed — and we may
well ask, if such testimony, to which much more may be added,
can be reasonably or safely rejected? This evidence, full and
complete as it is, is all in one direction ; supports and is supported by the account of the occurrences referred to as written
by Paul Revere and printed in 1798 : The testimony of Mrs.
Swift, grand-daughter of Col. Conant, confirms the arrangement made with him, and that of Maria Green, grand-daughter
of Capt. Barnard, that made with Mr. Newman ; and all this,
uniform and conclusive as it certainly is, while there is not the
slightest authority, record or tradition, in support of the North
square meeting house, as the place where the lanterns were
shown ; nor the merest record or tradition, excepting that of the
Pulling family, (which remains to be considered,) but that
which, coming from ten or twelve different families, points
directly to Mr. Robert Newman, the sexton, as the friend of
Paul Revere, who displayed them.

VII.   THE PULLING TRADITION.

In July, 1876, in consequence of some statements made at
the Centennial celebration of the 18th of April, at Christ
Church, Rev. John Lee Watson, of New Jersey, published a
paper entitled, "the True Story of the Signal Lanterns in
Christ Church, Boston." It was then deemed to be a very bold
announcement, and it is now seen that the whole relation, like
its title, is remarkably pretentious and dogmatic. The writer
hardly recognizes the fact that there is such a thing as adverse
evidence to his statement, and in various other ways shows his
want of knowledge on the subject upon which he presumes to
write so positively. In the fourth line of his paper he speaks
of "the signal lanterns which directed the movements of Paul
Revere on that night," when the fact is just the opposite of this
statement. Paul Revere did not need signal lights to direct
his movements: he directed the signal lights for the information of others, in case he should be interrupted or seized: any
other statement is a perversion of the truth.

The exclusive object of this somewhat remarkable paper is to
claim for John Pulling, who it seems was a relative of the writer, the honor of having put up the lanterns. as against the
claim of Robert Newman. Speaking of Newman's claim, he
says, "*knowing* that this statement could not be correct," &c.,
and "believing the honor belonged rightfully to a member of
our family," &c.. he asked the Rev. Dr. Burroughs for a statement of the evidence in favor of Mr. Newman. After giving a
brief outline of the evidence furnished to him, and naming some

of the parties, he says, "this is all, and I have no occasion to make any remark upon their evidence." Thus ignoring without further remark, the accepted history of a hundred years.

He then proceeds to tell his own story, with the same degree of assurance, and in considerable detail, "derived," as he says, "principally from the letters of my kinswoman, the granddaughter of John Pulling," recently written, of course, and wholly traditionary. Her statements from memory are the basis of Mr. Watson's "knowing;" against which similar testimony from all the north end, as it were, is of no account: he *knows* everybody else is wrong because she told him! Yet she never heard the name of Mr. Newman before, and of course never could have heard the story before, as told at the north end, where it occurred. Mr. Fowle and others say they never heard of Mr. Pulling before, and Mr. F. says "it was well known at the north end that Robert Newman was the man."

Mr. Pulling, Mr. Watson states, was a vestryman,* and a friend of Paul Revere, and adds "they were both also the associates of Hancock, Warren, Adams, and other leading patriots." We discredit this last statement entirely, and do not hesitate to express the opinion that it is not correct. Paul Revere was employed by Dr. Warren and the patriots; was eminently useful to them, and his associates at this time, were the North end mechanics; but we do not recognize Mr. Pulling's name in connection with either party at this time, and certain it is that he was in no proper sense the associate of Hancock and Adams, or, we think, of Paul Revere and the North End mechanics. —

---

* John Pulling, Jr. was a vestryman in 1769, after his father, who died in 1771, aged 71. The son was born in February 1736, and died "soon after the siege was raised," and of course was not in the war which followed.

Mr. Watson also assumes that John Pulling was one of the
" thirty, chiefly mechanics," who held their secret meetings at
the Green Dragon ; or, ·if not so, that he was one of those to
whom their secrets might be divulged; these last, he says, were
" the committee chosen by themselves, to which Paul Revere
and John Pulling belonged." The mechanics never chose any
such committee, and John Pulling, a vestryman and a merchant,
was never admitted to their secrets as stated. Yet the author,
suppressing dates, hangs upon his erroneous statements a most
specious argument, as unjust as it is inaccurate. Two committees are mentioned by Mr. Watson, upon which the names of
Paul Revere and John Pulling appear : the first was a town
committee and the second a sub-committee of the same. Even
the appointment of these from the printed record, is not correctly stated. We quote the passage :

" I find also in the 'Records of the Boston Committee of Cor-
respondence, Inspection and Safety,' recently published for the
first time,* that he and Paul Revere are mentioned together as
'Captain John Pulling and Major Paul Revere,' and as chosen
members of that committee ; and from the titles given them it
may of course be inferred that they both held commissions in the
Continental service.† It is also recorded, that ' at a meeting of
the freeholders and other inhabitants of the town of Boston, in
public town meeting assembled, at the Old Brick Meeting
house,' &c., it was ' voted that Capt. John Pulling, Maj. Paul
Revere,' and others, ' be appointed a sub-committee to collect
the names of all persons who have in any way acted against or
opposed the rights and liberties of this country,' &c."

The reader will be surprised to learn that the committee first

---

* New England Historical and Genealogical Register, for July, 1876.

† We do not think either of them ever held such a commission.

named, and not its sub-committee, was elected by the inhabitants, and that both of them were chosen more than a year after
the lanterns were shown ; after the Green Dragon secret club
had done its work ; in fact, after the evacuation of the town by
Gen. Howe and the end of the war in Massachusetts.   The
committee comprised 27 members, including Adams, Hancock,
Greenleaf, Mackay, Cooper, Brown, Bradford, Pitts, Appleton,
Davis, Barber, Proctor, Boyer, &c., and they were elected on the
29th of March, 1776, at the old brick meeting-house ; and the
sub-committee on the 7th day of May following, at a meeting of
the general committee, in the Selectmen's chamber.   Of course
neither of them were chosen by or ever had any connection with
the Green Dragon mechanics. So that the argument based upon
this s'range anacronism, and the conclusion assumed to be derived from it, so far as Pulling is concerned, fall to the ground,
reflecting upon the fairness of the reverend author, and making
it certain that Newman was one of the Green Dragon mechanics, and the man employed by Paul Revere.   It is a little
doubtful if Pulling and Paul Revere knew each other at all,
especially as Pulling was out of town until after the evacuation,
and, as far as we can learn, never acted with the patriots prior
to March, '76, while Revere, on the contrary, was constantly
in their employment.

   In connection with this perversion of fact and argument, Mr.
Watson asks with remarkable confidence, if there is a man
living who would believe that Paul Revere violated his solemn
oath "by intrusting to the sexton of the church that secret
which he had sworn upon the Bible he would discover to no one
except to the committees, Warren, Hancock, Adams, and one or
two more?"   As we have said, there never was any such com-

mittee, previously to the date above mentioned, and when
the sub-committee named was appointed, Warren had been dead
for nearly a year, and the question, so confidently proposed,
has no possible application to the case.   We agree that Paul
Revere would not, and did not, "violate his solemn oath," as he
must have done had he divulged the secrets of the club to John
Pulling, who was never a member of it or its committees, but
who a year later, after the enemy had been driven out of the
country, may have served with Revere and others, upon a town
committee.   But the fact is, the signal lanterns were Revere's
private arrangement, and there is no reason to suppose the club
had anything to do with them.   The arrangement with Colonel
Conant and others at Charlestown, was made only two days before the lanterns, and was no doubt known to Warren, Newman,
Capt. Barnard, the two men who rowed him across the river,
and Col. Conant and his friends at Charlestown.   If Revere or
Newman considered it necessary to have the consent of the wardens or vestrymen of the church, to the display of the lanterns, possibly Pulling may have been privy to it, and this
may afford an explanation of the family tradition.

Mr. Watson offers another argument, quite as absurd as that
which we have disposed of, viz : that the Rector having been
dismissed, rendered it "easy for Mr. Pulling, a vestryman,
to have entire control of the building," &c.   In this case did
not the Wardens have authority, and would not both rely upon
the sexton ?   Besides, the lanterns were shown on the evening
of the dismissal, before the excitement among the officials of the
church had subsided; and immediately after the signals, Mr.
Pulling, according to his relative, made his escape to Nantasket,

and was not heard of again until after the evacuation. So that he probably never had control of the building for an hour.*

There are other statements of Mr. Watson that seem entitled to consideration. His kinswoman writes that she "has heard the story from her earliest childhood," and adds " *I know* that he held the lanterns that night." This is rather positive testimony for one who was not born for some twenty years after the event affirmed. No doubt she "heard the story," as Mr. Watson says he did from his mother and aunt, and he finally sums up the whole in these words, " We have the evidence of family tradition that John Pulling was *the* friend of Paul Revere." This tradition, however honestly handed down as related, is at once met by the numerous adverse family traditions which we have given, and there are still more of them.

Mr. Watson adds to the above, "if the probabilities in the case are considered, I think they will sustain the family traditions." It is gratifying, considering the authoritative manner assumed in presenting the Pulling claim, to meet this sensible observation. If all the probabilities were as the writer supposes, and as he states them, the argument would be stronger, but they are not so : the relations between Revere and Pulling were not at all as claimed, and there is not the shadow of authority for the strong assertion, put in italics at that, that they " *always*

---

* Dr. Byles's Dismissal. The " Records of the Proprietors of Pews," show that "April 17, 1775, a committee waited on Dr. Byles to know if he intended to leave the church." "Tuesday, April 18, 1775," they report that Dr. Byles said, " For my part I am willing to give up the keys and quit the church, and hope they will pay me the balance due from the church."

The meeting accepted his resignation and sent a committee to inform him of their action, who came back and reported that Dr. Byles was contented with the proceedings.

acted together." We doubt if they ever "acted together" in the sense intended, until after the evacuation. Beyond all question Newman's relations to Revere, to the Green Dragon associates, and to the church, pointed him out as the instrument to be employed, just as Revere was the man of all others for Dr. Warren to select as his messenger. The disparaging remarks, twice repeated, against Mr. Newman are unjust, as we have shown,* and in very bad taste. As far as the two men are concerned, there is no reason for Revere's intrusting the service to Pulling rather than to Newman. Indeed, Pulling himself, who probably could not have "climbed to the upper window of the steeple" in the day time, was much more likely to engage the sexton, than to attempt such a thing himself in the darkness of night, even if Revere had applied to him, to do it.— It is not to be supposed for a moment that Revere did not know which man to employ.

Mr. Watson, from want of information on the subject, we are disposed to believe, permits himself to make some absurd and extravagant remarks, such as the following : "This, of course, was the most critical and hazardous part of the whole enter-

---

* Mr. Fowle, who knew Robert Newman personally, says on this point,— "The slur on Mr. Newman is, to say the least, an error. Mr. Newman, as well as Paul Revere, was educated at Mr. Tileston's school, and like Mr. Revere, was a mechanic. All sextons in those days were active and intelligent men. Mr. Newman was a man of few words, but prompt and active, capable of doing whatever Paul Revere wished to have done." Of what he says on this subject, Mr. Fowle has the right to use the words, " *I know.*"

In order to show how Mr. Newman was estimated by the church it may be mentioned that in 1791, after many years service, a vote of thanks by the Pew holders is recorded, as given to Mr. Newman, and his further assistance desired. The same vote is repeated and his pew tax is remitted for several years to 1801, and he was reported as present at the meetings in 1802 and 1803.;

prise. It was full of difficulty and danger." * * "He," meaning Mr. Pulling, "went to the church, locked himself in; and, climbing to the upper window of the steeple, he there *waited for a favorable moment*, and then *hung out* the signal of two lanterns," &c.

As to this being "the most hazardous part of the whole enterprise," (although it has nothing to do with the question,) the statement is an exaggeration; the service, whatever its risks, is not to be compared with that which Revere took upon himself to perform. The lanterns were of great importance in the event of his captivity, and his ride through the night was full of peril. The "climbing to the upper window of the steeple," with lanterns in his hands, would no doubt be difficult to one not familiar with the way; but the idea of "waiting for a favorable moment," at that height and time of night, is a trifle superfluous.* As to the streets of the North end being "full of danger that night," and "North square the most dangerous of all," we are not aware of any reliable evidence to authorize the statement; but, whether there were troops in North Square or not, it is certain that lanterns in "the North church steeple, towards Charlestown," could not have been seen from that point.† The

---

* The Rev. William Gordon, speaking of this night in a letter to a gentleman in England, says, "on the first of the night, *when it was very dark*, the detachment," &c.

† The "Letters of John Andrews," (Historical Collections,) contain the following items in relation to troops at the North End:

1774, December 30. "The marines, consisting of about 500 men, landed this forenoon, and have gone into barracks at the extreme part of the North End, by much the fittest place for them."

1775, January 11th. "This morning the soldiers in the barracks opposite movements of the troops were conducted as quietly as possible, and what excitement there was, was in the neighborhood of the common.   Mr. Fowle says, " No British soldiers ever paraded at the North part of Boston.   There was only one company at Copps' Hill.   North End was no place for display : they were likely to be interfered with."

REPORTED ARREST OF MR. NEWMAN.

There is nothing further in the Pulling story deserving consideration, excepting the account of the arrest of Mr. Newman and the escape of Mr. Pulling.   When the British heard of the signals in the church steeple, they naturally inquired for the sexton, and the Rev. Dr. Burroughs says " they found him in bed, arrested him and threw him into jail ; but he had taken such wise precautions that nothing could be proved against him, and he was set at liberty."   Mr. Watson, we know not on what authority, says he declared that he had given the keys of the church to Mr. Pulling and went to bed again, and that this answer procured his release.   If the matter was considered in a serious light and ever came before any proper tribunal, it is not very likely that such an answer would procure the release of the suspected party ; but we are not told who arrested or who released him, and we know of no record of any such proceeding. Mr. Pulling having been warned, it is said by Mr. Watson, effected his escape to Nantasket with his family, and remained

our house, left it and took quarters with the Royal Irish, in Gould's Auction Room or store, in the street leading to Charlestown Ferry."

Col. Heath's statement of 20th March, (ante, page 25,) would seem to show that these troops had been removed prior to April 18th.

away until "after the siege was raised." Mr. Watson adds, "he died soon after he returned to Boston."*

All we can say, as at present informed, is, that we doubt the accuracy of these statements, or whether in fact, Mr. Newman was arrested at all, and should like to be informed where Mr. Watson gets his information about Mr. Pulling's "watching his opportunity" and calling upon Mr. Newman for the "keys of the church," and the story of Mr. Newman's arrest, especially as his relative from whom he gets the tradition, never heard of Mr. Newman. As to Mr. Pulling's escape to Nantasket, where Gen. Gage could put his hand upon him at any moment, why should he not have joined the patriots at Cambridge, who would have protected him, if necessary, or if any pursuit had been made; but there is not a shadow of evidence of any attempt to arrest Mr. Pulling or any indication given that the matter, if known to the British authorities, was regarded as an offence to be punished by law; and as to the story of his escape with his family in a vessel carrying beer to a man-of-war in the harbor, or in a skiff, (which are the adverse statements,) they are too absurd for belief. No gentleman, we venture to say, unless bereft of reason, would so expose himself; nor was there any occasion for his continued absence, as far as appears. We repeat, we doubt the whole story, and regard the evidence already given that "Robert Newman was the man" who held out the lanterns, as conclusive and satisfactory and not to be again disturbed.

---

* Mr. Watson appears to be wrong, as to the birth and death of Pulling, in both particulars: He says he was born February 18, 1737, when the clerk's record shows that he was baptized February 27, 1736, and instead of dying soon after he returned to Boston, was a vestryman until 1786.

VIII. CONCLUDING REMARKS.

In view of what has been said in these pages, there can be no doubt as to the purpose of the signal lanterns, or as to the place where they were displayed, if indeed there can be any as to the "friend of Paul Revere," who displayed them. It seems to the writer as if the evidence on all these points was clear and sufficient to place them beyond further question.

The moving spirit of the whole, however, was Dr. Joseph Warren, who a month before had delivered his eloquent oration on the Boston massacre, and two months later gave up his life on what by his sacrifice became the altar of his country. The importance of his services at this time, which were self-imposed, can scarcely be exaggerated, and so far seem not to have been fully appreciated, if indeed generally known.

Dr. Warren had remained in Boston to observe the movements of Gen. Gage, and was the only one of the patriots in town whom the mechanics could consult, or to whom they could communicate their observations and proceedings. During the time, more than three weeks, that the Provincial Congress and the Committee of Safety were in session at Concord, Warren was absent from all their meetings, and prompted all that was done to keep the patriots informed of the movements and purposes of Gen. Gage in Boston, and to him and Paul Revere, as his messenger, belong the honor of alarming the country in season to save most of the cannon and stores at Concord, and meet the enemy in that conflict which did so much to arouse and unite the colonies in the momentous conflict which followed.

Had this been otherwise ; had not Warren remained in Boston, to observe the movements of the British ; had not the country been warned and the people aroused, and had Gen. Gage's soldiers been allowed to do his bidding without hindrance, who shall say what the consequences might have been, temporarily perhaps, to the cause of the country !

The signal lanterns were projected by Revere to carry out the wishes of Dr. Warren, in case any obstacle should occur to prevent him from crossing the river, and at the same time covered any contingency that might occur to William Dawes, who had preceded him on the same errand over Boston Neck. The merit and wisdom of the lanterns, manifested in the foresight which suggested them, belong exclusively to Paul Revere, as the value and importance of the whole proceeding does to the constant devotion and presence of mind of Dr. Warren.

CONCLUSIONS.

1. That the Signal Lanterns, on the 18th of April, 1775, were in pursuance of an arrangement between Paul Revere and Colonel Conant and other gentlemen at Charlestown.

2. That the lanterns were shown in *" the North Church steeple,"* (or *Christ Church,*) and not in the " old North Meeting-house," in North Square.

3. That the lanterns were shown by Robert Newman, sexton of the church, and the friend of Paul Revere.

NOTE. The use of the word ' playmates," in speaking of Revere and Newman, on page 33, is an inadvertency—Revere was seventeen years his senior.

HISTORICAL INACCURACIES,

CONNECTED WITH THE 19TH OF APRIL.

———

The Pictorial History of the American Revolution, published in 1877, says, on the 18th of April Gen. Gage embarked 800 men "on Charles River, at Boston Neck. They sailed *up the river*, landed at Phipps' Farm, and advanced toward Concord." p. 140. The troops embarked at the foot of the common and crossed the river down the stream.

The Student and Schoolmate, vol. 23, 1869, says, "When in April, it was known to the committee of safety that the British were to march to Lexington, *where the patriots had collected military stores*," &c. There were not any military stores collected at Lexington.

A volume "From the Hub to the Hudson," published in 1869, speaking of Concord, says, "any one will show you the road that leads to the spot where, on the 19th of April, 1775, the revolutionary war began. *The day before*, at Lexington, the American militia had been fired on by Pitcairn's British regulars," &c. On the next page the author says, "If they had known what had happened the day before at Lexington," &c. Such glaring inaccuracy, it is not too much to say, is entirely inexcusable.

Lossing, in his "Pictorial Field Book of the Revolution," states among other things, that "Paul Revere and William Dawes had just rowed across the river to Charlestown," and in his later work, "Our Country," he adopts the mistakes of the poet, and keeps Revere waiting for his own signals in the presence of those for whose information they were made and who had seen them.

Errors of the description of those mentioned have multiplied indefinitely, and are to be found where they should not occur. Rev. Mr. Watson repeats the remark that the signal lanterns were for "the guidance of Revere," and the Lexington centennial "Souvenir" makes the same mistake. Revere knew more than the lanterns could tell, and when he got across the river, he says, "I told them what was acting, and went to get me a horse."

REVOLUTIONARY MEMORIALS.

PREFATORY REMARKS.

The expiration of a century since the beginning of " that train of events which led to the American Revolution," and the independence of the country, naturally directed the public attention to those points in the city proper and its immediate neighborhood where some of the most important of those events occurred, and led to the wish that they should be designated in some appropriate manner as landmarks in the local history of the city. With this purpose in view the City Council of 1876 took action in the matter which has resulted in the erection of three memorials, one in Roxbury, one on Dorchester Heights, (South Boston,) and the third, the Tablet now upon the tower of Christ Church.

The monument at Roxbury High Fort and that at Dorchester Heights were erected by order of the City Council of 1877, and the tablet on Christ Church, as has been stated, by that of 1878. They are simple and suitable memorials of the important incidents which they commemorate, and the tablet on the venerable church, the oldest public building,* (except the Province House), now standing in Boston, is a worthy monument to the memory and services of Paul Revere.

---

* The dates of the pre revolutionary buildings now standing are as follows :

Province House,	-	-	- 1679	Old State Ho., 1657, pres. edifice, 1748
Christ Church,	-	-	- 1723	King's Chapel, 1688, " " 1749
Old South, 1669, present edifice, 1729				Faneuil Hall, 1742, " " 1763

I. TABLET ON CHRIST CHURCH.

THE interesting incident of Paul Revere's Signal Lanterns having been established as related in these pages, the contemplated purpose of the City Government of 1876, in relation to the place where they were shown, has been accomplished by that of 1878. The Tablet, or block of granite, which has been placed upon the tower of *Christ Church*, on Salem street, to commemorate the incident, is 10 ft. 8 inches in length by 6 ft. 4 inches in width, and one foot in thickness. It is placed 42 feet above the sidewalk; the letters are 6 and 8 inches in height, and the inscription may be easily read from the street.

There has been for some years past, a question as to the real *purpose* of the signal lanterns, mainly growing out of the mistakes of the poet, and this, in view of what has been done towards correction, may well deserve a moment's consideration. It was very natural to suppose that the signals were made for Paul Revere and that he was waiting on the opposite shore. This *inference* was incorporated as history into the poem of Mr. Longfellow, who has said that "he found the incident [of the lanterns] mentioned in a magazine, and that it gave him the idea of the poem." Since the poem was published, the popular belief has conformed to its teachings, so much so that the committee of the City Council, in 1876-7, appear to have accepted the poet's version as veritable history, and proposed the following inscription for the tablet : "The lanterns hung from this tower signalled to Paul Revere the march of the British troops upon Concord and Lexington."

When this appeared in print, the writer having already taken some interest in the subject, addressed a note to Mayor Pierce, suggesting that the proposed inscription was "inaccurate and untruthful," and hoping that it would be corrected before being put in place. Not having had his attention called to the subject the Mayor handed the note to the City Clerk, who replied, "that the inscription was ordered by vote of the City Council, after a hearing upon the subject, and cannot be changed except by a similar vote authorizing such change," and suggesting that others had desired to substitute "the Patriots" for "Paul Revere," which he regarded as merely technical.

Believing such an inscription a perversion of history, and the perpetuation of an error, for which in view of Paul Revere's own relation, there could be no excuse, we could not hesitate to make a still more earnest effort for its correction, even though the tablet, as we were told, had been executed. Thereupon, we addressed a second letter to Mayor Pierce:

" Concord, (Mass.) March 23, 1878.

" Dear Sir, I trust you will allow me to acknowledge to you the receipt of a note from the City Clerk in answer to mine of the 20th, addressed to you. If, as he understands, my objection (so to speak) was merely technical, it would perhaps have been undeserving any answer. My statement was that the proposed inscription was both "inaccurate and untruthful," and if you will allow me, I will specify the points wherein it is so. The lanterns were in no sense signals *to* Paul Revere, but, on the contrary, were *his* signals to Col. Conant and others, at Charlestown, made by special agreement between them, and the statement is therefore inaccurate and untruthful. Paul Revere did not see them; *they were not made for him*, and he did not need to see them. They did not signal to him the "march of the British troops," for he knew of the movement before he left

Boston. The *sole object* of the signal lanterns was to alarm the country of the movement of the British troops, (through Col. Conant and other gentlemen,) in case he (Paul Revere), should be seized or otherwise prevented from crossing the river to give the alarm himself, and carry Dr. Warren's message to Lexington. I repeat, they were in no sense signals *to* Paul Revere, ' while on the opposite shore,' as the poet says, but his signals to the gentlemen mentioned, and we now know would have accomplished their purpose by his foresight in the matter, had he been seized or upset in the river. If these things are so, is not the proposed inscription ' inaccurate and untruthful,' and should it not be revised and corrected ?

" Allow me to add a brief word of criticism. The proposed inscription, if my copy is correct, says ' march of the British troops *upon* Concord and Lexington.' The use of the preposition ' upon,' I think, is objectionable, and the sentence reads as if we should say, in another case, ' the Massachusetts troops marched upon Washington and Baltimore.' "

" I trust your Honor will excuse what may seem to be meddlesome on my part, in addressing a second note to you on this subject ; but it impresses me very strongly that the perversion of history in putting up such an inscription cannot be in accordance with the character of the people of Boston. I may add that I have no personal interest in the matter, or any connection with those who may have, and am prompted only by the interest which I feel in my native city, in which, in my boyhood, I was permitted to drive my mother's cow to our pasture on Boston Common. Very respectfully," &c.

In connection with the delivery of this letter, Mayor Pierce indulged the writer in a partial hearing of the matter, in the presence of the Chairman of the Board of Aldermen, President of the Council, City Clerk, Architect, and other members of the government: and the same evening, by the prompt action of these gentlemen, an order was passed by the Board of Aldermen, and subsequently by the Common Council, authorizing His Honor the Mayor to correct the inscription. In doing this it became necessary to re-write it, and owing to the position it was to occupy, to make it as brief as possible. The necessity for the signal lanterns arose from the fact that Dr. Warren wished Revere to carry a message to Hancock and Adams, to warn them and the country, when the British troops should march to seize the stores and ammunition at Concord. Fearing it might not be possible to cross the river, when this message became necessary, Paul Revere, on his return from Lexington, on the previous Sunday, (April 16th), made an arrangement with Colonel Conant and other gentlemen at Charlestown, to convey the information to them by means of one or two signal lanterns in the steeple of the North Church; and this necessity arose on the evening of April 18, 1775. As it was impossible to include all these circumstances in the inscription, the language adopted is as follows :

THE SIGNAL LANTERNS OF
PAUL REVERE,
DISPLAYED IN THE STEEPLE OF THIS CHURCH,
APRIL 18, 1775,
WARNED THE COUNTRY OF THE MARCH
OF THE BRITISH TROOPS TO
LEXINGTON AND CONCORD.

The Tablet was placed in position without any ceremony of inauguration on the 17th of October, 1878.

II. ROXBURY HIGH FORT.

THE Monument at Roxbury is on the site of the old fort at Highland Park. When Gen. Washington took command of the troops around Boston. July, 1775, he found, as he says, a complete line of circumvallation from Charles River to Mystic River, and at Boston Neck, he said, "Our people have intrenched across the outer end, and are strongly fortified there and on the hill near the meeting-house" — referring to the fort which had been built there — one of several in the line.

Dr. Belknap, speaking of the fortifications at Roxbury, October, 1775, says "a wall of earth is carried across the street to Williams' old house, where there is a formidable fort, mounted with cannon." Finch, in his account of "Forts around Boston," says, "The lowest fort in Roxbury appears to have been the first erected, and by its elevation commanded the avenue to Boston over the peninsula, [Neck], and prevented the advance of British troops in that direction. *   *   On a higher eminence of the same hill is situated a quadrangular fort, built on the summit of a rock, and being perhaps the first attempt at a regular fortification, it was considered by the militia of unparalleled strength, and excited great confidence in that wing of the army stationed at Roxbury."

Cannon were placed in this fort at the time of its construction, and the first shot, it is said, were thrown from them into the town, on the first of July, the day before Washington reached Watertown. The next day the British returned the fire from the lines on the Neck.

MONUMENT AT HIGHLAND PARK,

ROXBURY, 1877.

The Monument is about 6 feet in height and 4 feet wide, in the form of a mounted tablet, with a cannon at each end and balls on the top, all of granite, elevated on a mound of earth.

The following is the inscription :

ON THIS EMINENCE STOOD

ROXBURY HIGH FORT,

A STRONG EARTHWORK PLANNED BY
HENRY KNOX AND JOSIAH WATERS,
AND ERECTED BY THE AMERICAN ARMY
JUNE, 1775, CROWNING THE FAMOUS
ROXBURY LINES OF INVESTMENT AT THE
SIEGE OF BOSTON.

III. DORCHESTER HEIGHTS.

THE second Monument is at Dorchester Heights, South Boston. The occupation of Dorchester Heights was one of the most brilliant and effective achievements of the war. It was originally proposed by the Committee of Safety, at the time of the occupation of Bunker Hill, when it was understood to be the purpose of Gen. Gage to do so ; but the battle of Bunker Hill prevented the movement by either party, and the position remained unoccupied during the year. In February, 1776, the river and harbor being frozen over, a Council of War was called to consider the plan of attacking the British over the ice. This plan had long engaged the attention of Washington, but was at once deemed unfeasible, and then was renewed the proposal to occupy Dorchester Heights, for which preparations had already been made. The proposition was at once adopted by the Council, and on the evening of the 4th of March, after a cannonad-

ing from other points for the two preceding days, the heights
were occupied, and before 10 o'clock, on the morning of the 5th
of March, the works were completed and manned.   Gen. Heath
says, " Perhaps there never was so much work done in so short
a time," and Gen. Howe was astonished and declared that his
" whole army could not have accomplished so much work in a
month."   The "novel mode of defence" around these works,
which made them unapproachable, was suggested by a Boston
merchant, and is described in a letter to the writer from a gentleman in Texas, who heard the story from Rev. Oliver A. Shaw,
told to him when a boy, by his grandfather in Cambridge :

" Twenty-five hogsheads filled with earth and stones, were
placed on the brow of the hill, and each secured by a single
stake driven into the ground in front, in such a manner, that,
as soon as it was removed, the hogshead would begin to roll
down.   One man [and Mr. Shaw said his grandfather was one
of them,] was placed at each hogshead.   When the red-coats
were half-way up the hill, the stakes were to be drawn, and
each man to give his hogshead a kick, and start it forward, and
then run for the fort."   The hogsheads, or barrels, accomplished
their purpose, as no army could have gone up in face of them.

The fort commanded the town and the harbor.

The following is the inscription on the monument :

LOCATION OF THE AMERICAN REDOUBT,

ON

DORCHESTER HEIGHTS,

WHICH COMPELLED THE EVACUATION

OF BOSTON BY THE BRITISH ARMY

MARCH 17, 1776.

HISTORY OF THE CONCORD FIGHT.

IT is not very remarkable, perhaps, that the centennial period since the beginning of the revolutionary war should be the occasion of bringing to light some new matter in relation to its early incidents, in regard to which more or less secrecy was preserved and names withheld at the time. It seems from evidence which has lately come to the knowledge of the writer, by a casually dropped remark, concerning the Concord Fight, that the alarm of the movement of General Gage, to seize the cannon, stores and ammunition in that town, was more widely spread in Middlesex county than heretofore supposed. It appears from the testimony of Mr. Artemas Wright, of Ayer, who is a grandson of Mr. Nathan Corey, of Groton, that there were several members of the Groton company of Minute men at Concord on the morning of the 19th of April, who were in the fight at the North Bridge and joined in the pursuit of the British troops in the retreat to Lexington. Mr. Wright says his grandfather told him the story and often talked of the scenes of that day.

His narration was that on the day before, April 18, while he was ploughing in his field, some distance from the middle of the town, he received notice of a meeting of the Minute men, which of course demanded immediate attention. It was towards evening when he received the notice. He at once drove his oxen home, took down his gun and powder horn, (which latter was preserved by Mr. W. for many years, until it was destroyed in the burning of his house), told his wife Molly that he was going away and did not know when he should come back, lighted a pine torch (for the roads at this time went by marks on the trees,) and went to the middle of the town. The news, which

was before them in the shape of brass cannon, and the subject
of going to Concord, were talked over, and the company voted
not to march that night.   This, it seems, was not the disposition of all the members, and some of them determined to go at
once, and nine of them, with young Corey among them. started
for Concord, travelled all night and reached there at an early
hour in the morning. entering one side of the town some hours
before the British troops entered on the other.   Mr. Corey said
they all went and got some breakfast at the house of Col. Barrett, which was afterwards visited by British troops in search of
cannon and stores, most of which had been removed to places of
safety.   After getting something to eat, they proceeded towards
the centre of the town and finally joined the men of Concord at
or near the Bridge, where the fight occurred.   They continued
with the minute men and followed the retreating troops.

This story, according to the accepted history of the time, appears to be wholly improbable, and must remain so unless it can
be explained. as we think it can be.   The objection to be met
and answered is, How could the people of Groton, 30 miles from
Boston, at the time the British troops were moving towards
their boats, know anything of Gen. Gage's purpose, or design
to visit Concord ?   This is the matter to be explained after the
lapse of more than a century.

It is well known to readers who are familiar with the history
of this period that Dr. Warren sent a message by Paul Revere
to Hancock and Adams. at Lexington, on Sunday, April 16th,
1775, that the British were preparing for an excursion into the
country, and it was at once understood that the stores and ammunition collected at Concord. were the object.   Revere delivered his message and returned on Sunday night.   On Monday
morning the Committees of Safety and Supplies, at Concord.
(not having adjourned when the congress did), commenced their
session before Hancock arrived.   They voted that Col. Barrett
should mount some cannon. form an artillery company and employ a teacher ; and then voted to adjourn to Wednesday morning.   After this, it is supposed, Hancock arrived and communi-

cated the intelligence he had received from Dr. Warren.   The Committees then voted "that the four six pounders be transported to Groton and placed under the care of Col. Prescott," the representative from that town ; and other cannon were ordered to be sent to Acton for safe keeping.   (It will be recollected that only a short time before this, Gage sent Col. Leslie to Salem to seize some pieces of cannon there.)   The next day the cannon were on the way to Groton, and arrived there late in the afternoon of Tuesday, 18th, while the British troops were getting ready to embark at Boston.

It may now be pretty confidently asked, What message did the appearance of those cannon at Groton communicate to the minute men of that town ?   There cannot be a doubt as to the tale they told, even if the men who carried them had been speechless.   The proceedings which followed, as we have stated them, were both natural and reasonable, even supposing the volunteers moved by curiosity alone :   a mere desire to see British soldiers.   The minute men were promptly called together, and some of them determined to go to Concord that night; and while Col. Smith was moving his troops over the Cambridge marshes and swamps, these patriots were on their way to meet them at Concord Bridge and hang upon their rear in the retreat, which, we have no doubt, they did.

— Since the first publication of this matter, Dr. Samuel A. Green, a native of Groton, has published a handsome volume, illustrated, entitled "Epitaphs from the Old Burying Ground in Groton, Mass."   One of the inscriptions, found upon the monument to the memory of Capt. Abram Child, contains the following sentence :   "He was a Lieutenant among the Minute men, and aided in the Concord Fight and the Battle of Bunker Hill. 1775."   The remainder of the inscription shows that Capt. Child went through the war with Washington, and was the oldest captain in the service at the capture of Stoney Point, in 1779. He was just the man for a night expedition to Concord.

EVENTS AND MOVEMENTS OF THE EXPEDITION TO LEXINGTON AND CONCORD.

Prepared by William W. Wheildon.

SATURDAY, APRIL 15th, 1775.

Provincial Congress at Concord ; afternoon adjourned without day,

SUNDAY, APRIL 16th.

First message sent to Lexington by Paul Revere.

Evening : Revere's arrangement with Col. Conant for the lanterns.

MONDAY, APRIL 17th.

Committees of Safety and Supplies, at Concord ; artillery cannon ordered to Groton and Acton ; afternoon, adjourned to Menotomy.

TUESDAY, APRIL 18th.

Committees meet at 'Menotomy in the morning. and adjourn at sunset.

Evening : Devens and Watson meet British officers on the road, and then return to Menotomy, and send a message to Hancock.

9 o'clock, British troops moving from the common towards the river.

10 o'clock, William Dawes despatched over the Neck.

10.30, Troops in the boats. Revere despatched.

11, Signals seen. Revere across the river ; ready to start.

12 o'clock, British troops commence the march from Phipps' Farm.

" Revere at Clark's house in Lexington. Dawes arrives soon after.

WEDNESDAY, APRIL 19th.

1 to 2, A. M. Lexington alarmed ; minute men on the field ; Revere and Dawes start for Concord ; captured by British officers ; Prescott effects his escape and spreads the alarm to Concord.

5 o'clock, British troops fire upon and kill minute men at Lexington.

7 to 7.30, British troops enter Concord.

7.30 to 8, Americans retreat over the North Bridge to the high ground.

8, Reinforcements under Percy start from Boston.

9.30, Acton company arrive at Concord and join the minu'e men.

10, British troops at Col Barretts. Destruction of stores, burning cannon carriages, wheels, &c. in town. Alarm of fire.

" Dr. Warren rode through Charlestown. Gen Heath in the field.

11, Americans attempt to cross back over the bridge ; shots exchanged. Fight at the North Bridge ; British and Americans killed ; British retreat and join the main body.

12, British troops move from the town, followed and fired upon by the minute men.

12.30, fighting at Merriam's corner ; British soldiers killed.

2, P. M., met Percy's brigade of reinforcements at Lexington.

5 and 6, fighting at Menotomy. Danvers troops arrive and engaged.

6.30, Pickering's Regiment arrives near Prospect Hill, a little too late.

7 and 8, British arrive at Prospect Hill and reach Charlestown soon after.

9, 10, 11, boats of the Somerset removing the wounded across the river.

HISTORY

OF

Paul Revere's Signal Lanterns

APRIL 18, 1775,

IN THE

STEEPLE OF THE NORTH CHURCH:

WITH AN ACCOUNT OF

THE TABLET ON CHRIST CHURCH AND THE MONUMENTS AT

HIGHLAND PARK AND DORCHESTER HEIGHTS.

————— ◄•◆•► —————

BY WILLIAM W. WHEILDON.

———

WITH HELIOTYPE OF CHRIST CHURCH.

———

BOSTON :
LEE & SHEPARD, Publishers.
1878.

Inauguration of the Statue of Warren, by the Bunker Hill Monument Association, June 17, 1857, by Wm. W. Wheildon, Editor, with an engraving of the Statue and portrait of Thomas H. Perkins. 8vo. pp. 224. Boston, 1858.

Memoir of Solomon Willard. Architect and Superintendent of the Bunker Hill Monument. By William W. Wheildon. 8vo. with plates. pp. 288. Boston, 1865.

Contributions to Thought. By William W. Wheildon, Fellow of the A. A. A. S. 12mo. pp. 236. Concord, author's private print, 1875. $1.

New History of the Battle of Bunker Hill, June 17, 1775. Its purpose, conduct and result. By William W. Wheildon. 8vo. pp. 58. Lee & Shepard, Boston, 1875. 50 cents.

Siege and Evacuation of Boston and Charlestown, with a brief account of Pre-Revolutionary Buildings. By William W. Wheildon. 8vo. pp. 64. Lee & Shepard, 1876. 50cts.

Sentry or Beacon Hill: The Beacon and the Monument, of 1635 and 1790. By William W. Wheildon. 8vo. pp. 120. with maps, heliotypes and engravings. Paper 75 cts.

Letters from Nahant. Historical, Descriptive and Miscellaneous. By William W. Wheildon. 12mo. pp. 48, with engravings. Press of the Bunker Hill Aurora, 1848. 25c.

Arctic Regions. 1. Atmospheric Theory of the Open Polar Sea, with remarks on the Present State of the Question.— 12mo. pp. 34. 2. Atmospheric Theory of the Open Polar Sea and an ameliorated climate. 8vo. pp. 26. 3. The Arctic Continent, or Wrangell's Land, with government map.— By William W. Wheildon. Re-printed from volumes of the American Association for the Adv. of Science. 25 cts each.

Scientific Excursion Across the State of Iowa, from Dubuque to Sioux City and Springvale (Humboldt). 8vo. pp. 11. By William W. Wheildon. Concord, 1873.

The Maverick Bridge, (proposed). Argument before the U. S. Commissioners at the Charlestown Navy Yard, Sept. Oct. 1868. By William W. Wheildon. 8vo. pp. 40. Charlestown. Press of Bunker Hill Aurora.

The American Lobster, (Homarus Americanus). Natural History and Habits. By William W. Wheildon. 8vo. pp. 10. Concord, 1875. 25c.

Paul Revere's Signal Lanterns, April 18, 1775. By William W. Wheildon. 8vo. pp. 64. Concord, 1878.

Bunker Hill Aurora, weekly, May, 1827 to October, 1870, edited by Wm. W. Wheildon, Charlestown. [44 volumes in the Charlestown Public Library.]

Sent post-paid on receipt of price by LEE & SHEPARD, or by the author No. 2, State-st., Boston, or Concord, Mass.

BOOKS FOR LIBRARIES.

AMERICAN FICTION.

A Year Worth Living. By W. M. Baker, author of " The New Timothy," 'Carter Quarterman," etc. 12mo., cloth. $1.50.

His Inheritance, by Miss Adeline Trafton, author of "The American Girl Abroad," "Katharine Earle," etc. 12mo. cloth. $1.50.

An American Consul Abroad. By Samuel Templeton. 12mo. 1.50

Rothmell. By the author of 'That Husband of Mine,' 12mo. 1.50.

Blufftou. By Rev. Minot J. Savage, Pastor of the Church of the Unity, Boston. 12mo. cloth, $1.50.

The Fall of Damascus, by Chas Wells Russell, 12mo. cloth. 1.50.

Seola, an Anonymous Romance, 16mo. cloth, 1.50,

Quinnebasset Girls, by Sophia May, author of "Our Helen, The Doctor's Daughter, The Asbury Twins," etc. 12mo. cloth, $1.50.

From Hand to Mouth, by Miss A. M. Douglass, author of "Nelly Kinnard's Kingdom, In Trust," etc. 12mo. cloth, $1.50.

Ike Partington and his Friends, or the Adventures of a Human Boy, by R. P. Shillaber, small 4to. fully illustrated, $1.25.

A Paper City. A novel by Petroleum V. Nasby, cloth, $1.50.

A Woman's Word, and how she kept it, by Vir. F. Townsend. $1.50.

Burying the Hatchet, by Elijah Kellog, 16mo. illustrated, $1.25.

Live Boys, edited by Arthur Morecamp, 16mo. illustrated, $1.

HISTORICAL.

Young Folk's History of the United States. By Thomas Wentworth Higginson. Designed for home reading and the use of schools.— Square 16mo. pp. 380, over 100 illustrations $1.50.

Young Folk's Book of American Explorers, uniform with the above, by the same author. 16mo. cloth, illustrated, $1.50.

Vasco de Gama, the initial volume of a series of historical narratives for young folks, comprising the adventures of celebrated Navigators and Explorers, by George M. Towle. $1.

Pizarro, His Voyages and Adventures, by George M. Towle. Uniform with the above. 16mo. cloth, illustrated, $1.

Headley's Historical Library. 6 vols. illustrated, $1.50 per vol.
  The Island on Fire, a Thousand Years of the Old Northmen's Home, 874 to 1874, 12mo. cloth, illustrated.
  Life of the Empress Josephine, 12mo. elegant steel portrait.
  Life of Napoleon Bonaparte, 12mo. with portrait.
  Life of Mary Queen of Scots, 12mo. with handsome portrait.
  Life of Lafayette, 12mo. illustrated with portrait.
  Women of the Bible. 12mo. illustrated.

TRAVEL.

Over the Ocean, or, Sights and Scenes in Foreign Lands. By Curtis Guild, editor of Commercial Bulletin. Crown 8vo. cloth, $2.50.

Abroad Again, or Fresh Forays in Foreign Fields. Uniform with Over the Ocean. Crown 8vo. cloth, $2.50.

Voyage of the Paper Canoe, a Geographical Journey of 2500 miles, from Quebec to the Gulf of Mexico, during the year 1874-75. By Nath. H. Bishop, author of A Thousand Miles Walk across South America, with 10 maps and illustrations, crown 8vo. cloth, $2.50.

England from a Back Window, by J. M. Bailey. 12mo. $1.50.

Sold by all Booksellers and Newsdealers, and sent post-paid on receipt of price. Catalogues mailed free.

LEE & SHEPARD, Publishers, Franklin-st., Boston.

TRI MOUNTAIN AS SEEN FROM CHARLESTOWN IN 1630.

HISTORY OF BEACON HILL.

SENTRY, or BEACON HILL: The Beacon and the Monument of 1635 and 1790. By WILLIAM W. WHEILDON. Illustrated with Maps and Heliotypes. Author's private composition studio. 8vo. pp. 120. Concord, Mass. 1877.

OPINIONS OF THE PRESS.

" It contains a great deal of curious and valid historical information respecting what was once the most conspicuous landmark of Boston, and is illustrated with heliotypes," &c.—(Commonw'lth.

" A very interesting and truly valuable pamphlet. To Bostonians these accounts will be found particularly entertaining and instructive.—[Traveller.

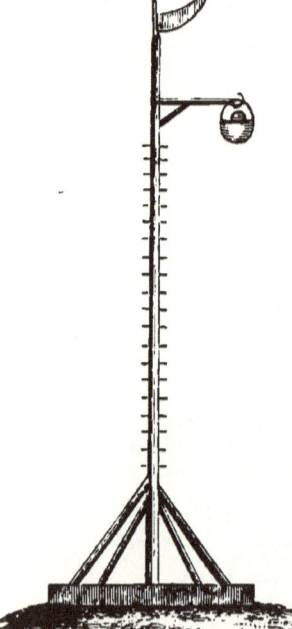

"As a monograph of local interest the volume is complete, and bears evidence of having been carefully prepared with the author's best skill and experience, and is replete with historical interest of a new and novel character.—(Sun. Her,

"It contains a full and valuable account of the early history of Boston, and is richly worthy of a careful perusal."—(Christian Watch.

"Historical students and those who for any cause are specially interested in Boston, will value highly this excellent monograph." — (Publisher's Weekly.

" Mr. Wheildon's full and careful monograph on Beacon Hill will at once commend itself to the attention of every one interested in the Boston of former generations."—[Daily Advertiser.